The Sensuous Overalls

Poems by Ove Wahlqvist

Illustrations by Matheo Yamalakis

Back cover photos taken on Zakynthos by
Lena Röpke and Ove Wahlqvist

Copyright 2013 Ove Wahlqvist
Förlag och tryck: BoD
ISBN: 978-91-7463-399-3

Alone in your sensuous overalls

Alone in your sensuous overalls
you contemplate the surroundings

Beneath layers of mud,
frozen roots and static stones
– a swift movement!
a mild warmth!

That's where you have to build!
in the evasive
in the barely perceptible

No architectural drawings are valid
no estimations
The construction firm vanished
like a mirage
The cranes were broken like matches

Alone in your sensuous overalls
you raise your yardstick

Vitamin shots

Vitamin shots
and jerky recoils

You cling to
the carousel,
try to feel which screws
will come loose first

And when the shot finally hits
you watch the ferris wheel
roll away

as if this was planned

I filled up your house

Your door cracked
I filled up your house
I broke the locks,
floated over the thresholds,
made a magic gesture
to soothe the flowers
I had told you
about my powers,
about the moment that would arrive
But you thought it was false alarm
once again
You thought there was time
You thought you could
postpone your decision
So now it is all completed
Now I live in your house
where everything is changed
Now you are a lodger,
a stranger
You rent on short-term basis,
can be evicted anytime
I am the host
I choose wallpaper,
furnishings, broadband connections

I decide which lamps
can burn all night
I decide when the door shall be locked
And you can just abide
You had your chance, and you blew it
You didn't understand the finality
of your choice
Now I will never ever stop talking
about all you have lost
You will hate me,
but you won't be able to get rid of me
Because I filled up your house
to the very last millimeter

And I'm sure
that the unexpected movement
I catch out of the corner of my eye
is not an up yours…?!

Next time I let you down

Next time I let you down
it's only for your own good
– to make you stronger,
to get you to understand life

The betrayal hurts me worst
It degrades me, makes me dirty,
makes me feel ashamed

But then again I know
it's only for your own good

What am I not capable of
to help another human being?!

You fell through the branches

You fell through the branches
Catching leaves and barque with your hands
as you went down
Heavy as basilica
with one single target: earth, roots
From high spaces
already with the underworld
in your veins

You were seen as an eagle
But you yourself knew, even up in the sky:
mud, groundwater, bedrock
Your air currents always came from the deep
Your wings faked the power to fly
but your mind was always wedged into the ground,
the worms already knew you

And I saw your fall
It was I who pulled away the safety net
Because we all have to fall freely

Now your weight lives
in the germination

The somersaults

The somersaults
– I do them for you!

The rocks were not there
before you made me seek
signposts, distance markers

I am all dried out,
the tracks of blood under the heather
wear your DNA

Once again I swing myself upwards

High above the heads of the audience
your womb is aglow

Don't split me up!

Don't split me up!
Save my original parts
Put me out on the yardsale by your back door
I'm sure there is some lunatic out there
who wants to recreate the past,
who once again wants to travel through
the inaccesible climes,
who wants to reach the border where
the possible ceases to exist

My worn out gear wheels will fit in there
By looking at them you can see how I used to function

But now I'm on sale

Buy my background vocals!
Buy my bass lines!
Buy the syncopes in my snare drum!

Buy me!

A yardsale is more then I ever expected

So don't split me up!
I am at my best in my own context
I am at my best when greedy hands flinch
before my unexpected wealth and hidden depths
I am at my best when silence vibrates in the details
I am at my best when I

Because I am the original
My gear wheels still know rotation
I still understand the machinery
and how the different parts must be oiled
to make the synapses work

My own self is unexpectedly indivisible
And I lie for a long time at the yardsale
by your back door
- glowing with happiness in spite of the fact
that no one wanted me

I am the Picasso of the yardsales
I know what I'm worth when the autumn storms
begin to moan and a cheese burger
is our smallest common denominator

I know what I'm worth

Indivisible I face a crying silence

– this is me, this is me, this is me!

In your scream

In your scream
I sow beauty

When your saliva decomposes
the theoretical arguments
I finally reach
the secret:

Saltiness, euphoria

Once again

Once again you head for Koltaluokta

Your steady hands lean on the wooden steering wheel
M/S Malla knows your slightest impulses
and you know hers

The visitors see a way to Treriksröset
You see the fascinating monotony
of the northern mountains
- the slopes change colours,
the clouds set up spontaneous theatre plays
above the grumbles of the dwarf birches

But the visitors are on their way
You are just a short stop in their journey
They want to incorporate Treriksröset
into their journey log

You steer your boat, bicker with the girls
in wandering boots,
hear the boys drop their cell phones into the cold water,
sink into the timetable and the eternal murmur,
notice how yet another couple of photos are
being taken by your everyday life
Then you land at the old Sami place
and the visitors trudge along on the only path

Later you pick them up and go back to Kilpisjärvi
– you are a reliable pendulum in the wilderness

When the poets write about the beauty of the barren
northern mountains you read their texts with a sly smile;
without your steady hand they would still be sitting
in the hotel bar, itching their mosquito bites
Now they have at least stumbled over the roots
on the path to Treriksröset

Posterity ows you a lot, but what do you care?
You just put another portion of snuff under your lip
and prepare the next departure

Soon there

The hedgehogs may well
float frozen speed bumps
in the mountain lake
as you once again
set out for
Koltaluokta

With your hands on
the wooden steering wheel you curse
their prickly spines' inability
to survive
But you love
their snouts who even in death
imbibe the beauty of the northern mountains

That's how you must live
– slightly late
That's how you want to die
– with sensitive surfaces
open to eternal slopes

Soon there!

<u>You get there faster!</u>

You get there faster!

You are already there!

Then you have to await
the official announcements
of your arrival

So that you become real
even to the blind

But you were there
a long time ago!

You have always
crossed the canyons
in a flash
– without a single
glance down!

Playing me

Playing me

The distance
between my outer
and my inner
face
is 28 meters

No more no less

Therefore the short breaks
between the words

Therefore the streak of desolation
in my gaze

Playing me

29

or possibly 27?

Never playback

Everything happens here
painfully now
– never playback!

Naked on the stage
you catch me in
the spotlight's circle

Everything happens now
painfully here
– never ever playback!

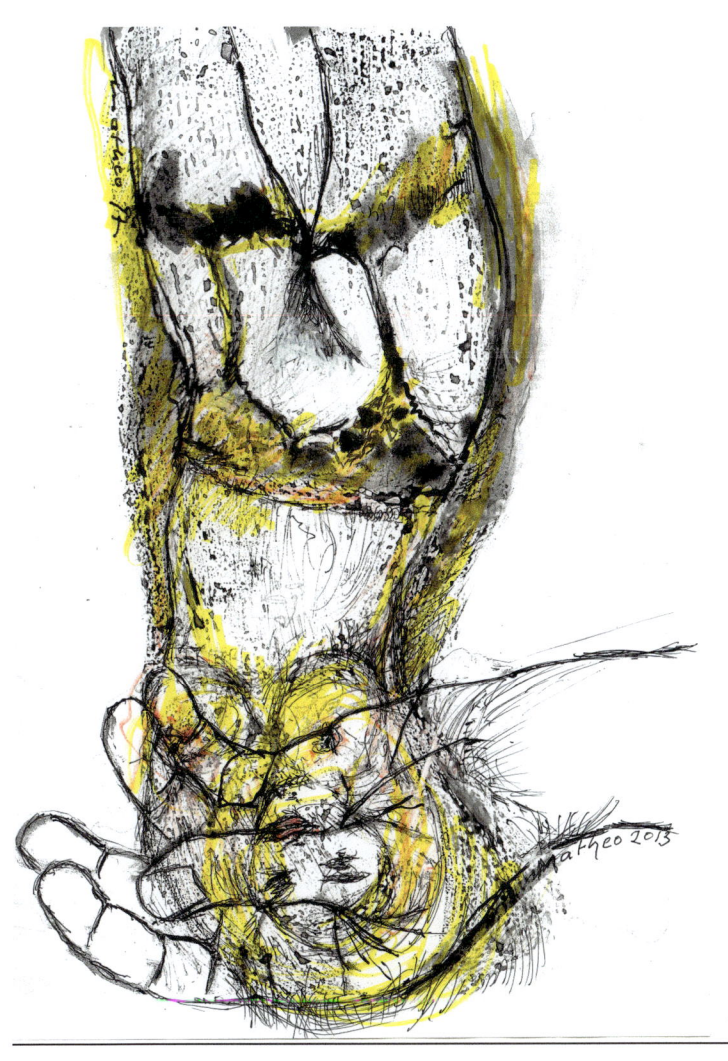

- 25 -

Camouflage

I am getting better
at camouflage

Did you notice the faint shift
in the backlight?

That was me

<u>Noncelebrity</u>

Noncelebrity

I blend in with the pulp

Did you see the faint ripple
in the cellulose factory's cistern?

That was me

Depression

Help, someone's coming!

Take on a face
Mount hands
Install a heart
Connect vocal cords
Raise a smile

There you go

Only the weak squeaking sound
betrays me

Death

Death
is a shameless
scoundrel

Coming here
offering me his shitty
eternity

I seriously consider
ending our
acquaintance

Some years after your death

Some years after your death
I met you
by the subway station

You looked a bit worn

As if the whole thing
had been nothing but a cruel,
exhausting joke

Our eyes did not meet

None of us wanted to know

@ugust Strindberg

You sure would have tweeted, @ugust!
You would have fought endless blog battles!
By the slightest injustice done to you
cyber space would have trembled with your wrath
By the mildest violation your enemies would
have felt your web hatred
Your PC keys would be dirty, some letters
totally worn out, and the virtual keyboard
on your cell phone smeared with sweat,
turpentine and ammonia
You would have reacted upon every provocation, started
facebook groups in your sleep,
constructed brilliant hashtags that were easy to find on
Twitter, spent days in front of the computer screen like a
teenager addicted to PC games, but of course with
much nobler aims
You would have found the code to hack your enemies'
accounts, you would have planted fiendish viruses and
trojans into the computers that belonged to the people
who thought they were your friends, but who at some
occasion had chosen the wrong word or the wrong path,
and thereby immediately had become your bitter enemies
You would as @rvidfalk instagram sumptuous views
over Stockholm seen from the Mosebacke Square, and
then slowly walk down the stairways, enjoying a cigarr
while the characters of your novel The Red Room were
born in your brain

You would be standing in the sunshine on Skeppsbron,
watching the socialists demonstrate on the First of May,
chanting your own slogans, and then head for your
regular table at the Berns restaurant
You would have googled alchemical formulas, and made
countless changes in Wikipedia articles about science,
occultism and obscure philosophers
You would have looked up all existing web pages about
Swedish history, and found the magical command to
delete the pages that didn't correspond to your own
analysis of the society
You would have mocked the feminist movement, and
dreamed nightmares about women taking over, but you
wouldn't feel at ease with your male artist friends in the
sauna either

And you would, like always, sneer at your wife Siri when
she tried to stop you from wasting your brilliant talent on
stupid intrigues and windmills

You would have run away to Paris with your PC as your
only luggage, checked in at the Pension Orfila, and then
written all through the nights like a maniac to deaden
the knocks on the walls
You would have experimented with synthtetical drugs,
mixed absinthe with amphetamine and shown your artist
friends in Grez-sur Loing films from
Andy Warhol's The Factory

You would have hated black metal, but still in secrecy
you would have envied the music its deadly energy, its
lack of compromises
You would zap around between 83 channels
and dismiss 81
You would have hated Usama bin Ladin
like a sick spleen,
but still you would like to seek him up in his cave to
discuss over a water pipe
You would have embraced and estimated the whole
digital evolution, but in secrecy you would see it as an
attack on your own well elaborated life wisdom
You would adapt some parts of "Hemsöborna" when the
mobile network reached Kymendö, but you would not
change Carlsson's Höganäs jar
You would have done so very much, and internet would
have been at your mercy

Yes, you sure would have tweeted and blogged, @ugust!
And if you weren't satisfied with what your own wrath
could accomplish you would have kidnapped millions of
computers and spammed all institutions, from royal
houses to multinational companies with dubious morals
Tour tweets would smell like fire, and sting like wasps
in a world finally adapted to your choleric,
blazing and lethal talent

@ugust – for you 140 characters would have been more
than enough!

Wordfeud

I only had three letters left
one of them an X

But still I played
PREDATORINESS
and won the game

At least morally

<u>The wheels of the wheelchair</u>

The wheels of the wheelchair now locked

As if this should prevent me
from the leaps towards the sky, the tango slips
and the accounting piroettes!

Go ahead, just lock the wheels!

By the afternoon coffee break
one cup will echo vacantly

In Knivsta

In Knivsta
a man is burning objects
in his garden

It is a happy man

It is a happy man!

My God, let it be a happy man!!

Public document

I am a public document

The veins on my left wrist
are being published with war time captions
on the headlines at Trafalgar Square

If I sneeze a bolt comes loose under Burj Khalifa
and the arab spring stops
for a short, breathtaking second

If I fall asleep by the wheel Fukushima is threatened
by yet another partial meltdown

If I feel unfairly treated
cold shivers float through the corridors of fascism

Because it's all my fault

I am a public document

I am Gaius Julius Caesar
I am Otto von Bismarck
But I am also the woman who with the menstrual cramps
chafing in my groins saw my man
go to war for King Gustav II Adolf
one of those first beautiful autumn days 1631

The slightest drop of sweat on my forehead
floods the empires
The slightest silly, uncertain smile
shakes the power structures
in the vulnerable areas

But how can I be held accountable?
I just did what we always have been doing
Fought on
Suffered
Said "It's okay, I'm fine. And you?"

One day in November you saw me
stumble out into the rampant climes by Torne träsk

There went the history of the world - but you had no clue

My gray areas

Everything is fine

My gray areas just ache a bit
and sometimes I feel a sting in my hidden statistics
But besides from that everything is fine

Sure, sometimes I notice a vague discomfort
in my worst scenarios,
and yesterday I had to take two Aspirins
to soothe the pain in my analysises
But now everything is fine,
and my selection processes
are according to my doctor excellent
– at least for a man at my age

However, I must admit that I have been neglecting
my error sources lately
So I guess I have to do an effort
before too much of Nick's time has vanished
But I know Nick,
and I have learned to filter,
pan and refine time
- my pockets are filled with grains of gold
who at night shine through the worn trouser fabrics

So, everything is fine

I am a statistically correct creature
with just enough density for these surroundings
My windpipe interprets the oxygen atoms
without difficulty
My blood transports smoothly the important substances
around in my system
My skin fights bravely the radiation

Yes, everything would be perfect –
if it wasn't for that pain
in my gray areas and the sting in my hidden statistics
They make my causations a bit muddled
And when they call my name at the Bukowski auction
house the experts can never predict the bids

But raise a hand if you are in the room!

The Puttersmälla device (Big Bang)

You remember the puttersmälla of your childhood days –
the plastic or paper device that was attached to the
bicycle frame, and then hit the spokes with a sound that
made the small bicycle sound almost like a motorcycle
– that's how the sound can be
but perhaps a bit more muffled, mightier

But it's just that steady repetition
It's just those fast waves and that sound

Between every stroke billions of years pass

Every time the outcome is different;
sometimes The Roman Empire doesn't emerge,
sometimes the aquatic animals doesn't leave the sea to
live on land,
sometimes Jesus is called something else,
sometimes Buddha doesn't find his inner spiritual gifts

– but then again..! sometimes humanity reaches the point
where the slayer lays down his hand
and science and philosophy are joined together

The puttersmälla rattles on

You keep riding your bike through the well-known
streets of your childhood
happily unaware of the fact that the universe is being
recreated each time your worn sandals
push down the pedals

Haikus

Maundy Thursday sun

Maundy Thursday sun
skims the wintry springtime fields
– the growing is stored!

The wind turbines

The wind turbines stand
still in early morning sun
– enjoying their wait

Rickety gate

See a rickety gate
by the end of this wild road?
– dream on, dream further!

Totally still

Totally still in line
the columns of trees ramble
– rooted in escape!

Gray building anxiety

Gray building anxiety:
if the sun should intervene
like a crazy thought!

Between the lines

I read easily
between the lines, but I find
it hard to write there

Certain drops

Certain drops
don't even reach
their water

Your forehead
must be wide open
to receive them!

So fast, so light
– your senses just wriggle
for a millisecond
And then you are changed

The Zante poems

I am Swedish

I am Swedish
I stand here with the fee ready in my hand
I expect that the local bus
shall arrive to the stop in Argassi at 11.20
Because that's what it says on the sign

The sun rises even higher
and heats up the sea and tre streets
Artemis has gotten a cocktailbar of her own
I move the 50-, 20- and 10-cent coins around in my hand
to prevent them from getting too sweaty
Because I am Swedish
And it says 11.20 on the sign
The 4 wheeled motorbikes leave Olympic Rentals
and venture out onto the streets of Zakynthos
A tractor passes by Magic Mushroom Bar
as a modest reminder of a history,
a nearly totally hidden everyday life,
of people who haven't learned some Swedish phrases
to tempt tourists to enter bars that are open 24/7

Now it is 11.26
I am Swedish, and expect a loudspeaker voice to say

"The bus to Zante town is delayed due to a case of illness",
or to "traffic jam along the road"
But here are no loudspeakers
We wait
The sun gains even more territory
Artemis mixes her cocktails
I am Swedish
I wear the same Nike shoes as I did when it was minus 15
degrees and snow storm in Stockholm
Now my coins are getting more and more sweaty

I have appointments, people to meet!
I have video clips to capture!

The sun scorches
I am Swedish, but I can feel the Greek influence
sip into my blood
And I smile as yet another tourist
awkwardly drives away from Olympic Rentals

And lo and behold, here comes the bus!

I find a seat
and roll away in rattling airconditioned comfort
towards Zante town

Who is Swedish?
Who is Greek?
1,60 euros for the trip
Jamas, Artemis, jamas!

The 11.20 bus

Imagine if it wasn't the 11.20 bus
that arrived 11.32
but the 10.50 bus, or even 10.20
A breathtaking thought
that opens up undreamed of perspectives
What about if I can still catch
last week's plane to Barbados
or even the bus that took kids to the beach
outside of my Swedish hometown Eskilstuna
that warm summer day in 1963
What if the trains with departing friends
haven't yet left the stations
What if everything is still possible to change,
cancel or postpone
What if life's choices are still alive,
if the puzzle isn't finished
if pieces can change places
if another motif is possible

For how can you spot any difference
between the 11.20 bus and the 10.50?
Who knows the drivers schedules,
faces or names?
You just take your seat, and roll along
There is no way of telling by the seat's padding
if the bus is delayed by 12 minutes or 40 years

The houses and different views
that pass by keep their secrets
And how old am I, this philosopher by the window?
In spite of all the stamps and intricate patterns
in my ID card it could be just as false
and wrong as I myself sometimes am
when doubts and boredom rule my life

But still it was nice that the bus finally arrived!
They say my ticket is valid forever

Maybe I shall become a shopkeeper

Maybe I shall become a shopkeeper
on Tavoulari street in Zante town
I shall sit there outside my shop
and let all my hidden talents and instincts flourish
I shall sing "Stardust"
when a lady from Bremen passes by
Throw newly written poems
after the Norwegian family with three kids
Close my eyes and quiver like a maniac
when the minister from the European Council
wants to appear folksy
and negotiate with the locals
Maybe I shall surprise someone looking for bargains
by giving him the beautiful candelabra
in stylish brass for free
Maybe I shall discuss Platon's ideas
with the brittle little lady from the suburbs of Milano
Maybe I shall undress, dance naked in the street
and laugh together with the crowd
at all our human frailty

Yes, maybe I shall become a shopkeeper

If the world is ready…

Room 409

I am the lonely man in room 409
I watch TV programs on a language I don't understand
I discover thousands of letters in the uneven ceiling of the
hotel room
but I can't use them
I'm going to miss the barbecue tonight
Because I am the lonely man in room 409
The hissing sound of the air condition on 23 degrees C
makes me dream about Atlantic cruises
I seek coolness, serenity, rest for my soul,
a darkness that is soothing and not frightening
Because I am the lonely man in room 409
You may well plan your excursions
you may well grill your steaks
so that a gray haze encircles the pool bar
I won't be there
I have a life to balance
I have years to digest
I have needs to formulate
So you won't see me at the barbecue tonight
Because I am the lonely man in room 409
I eat a totally different meal
I drink another wine
I turn off the lamps early this night
and let another light sprinkle in through the curtains

I turn myself back to the point where my powers are stored
to restore them
and lock the door to room 409
for everyone who hasn't got the right key

Barbecue smell, and twilight
slowly falling over Zakynthos
– I am here! I am here! I am here!

Greece

Greece, your blue skies
your crackling motorbikes,
your souvenir stalls and your chaotic economy,
your demonstrations that seem distant on this island,
as if they were part of a reality show on TV

Here the birds are twittering and the tourists are tweeting
as if the world was idyllic and beautiful

A greek orthodox priest slowly walks along the street
What is he thinking?
What are his reflections on the tourists' colourful bathing suits
and their flip floppy beach sandals?

He leans for a while against a stone wall
and then continues his slow walk in an alternative universe
far away from Madonna's "Vogue" that booms out
from a powerful speaker system further down the street

Yes, Greece, you have many things to live up to
but you also get a lot for free

We barbarians visit, follow and support you

We are here if the Olympic Gods hit the wall

We raise our sunburnt arms
and worship you in the only way we can;
perhaps a bit phony, perhaps a bit simple -
with perhaps one too many uninterested glance
outside of your churches and monuments

But we do our best!

So welcome to our place sometime
– then we will wear our viking helmets
with big Scandinavian smiles!

The problem God

The problem is that you don't exist, God
The problem is that everything is
an eternally long evolution process
The problem is that you, God
wouldn't understand quantum physics
even if it was served to you on a plate
together with french fries and ketchup
– and that is remarkable
since it should have been you that invented it
Yes, the problem is you, God
You demand much, and appear in different shapes
You let your son get crucified
as if it was a loving father's normal way
of raising a child
You let yourself be chiselled out in countless altarpieces
Most of the time you have no problem with being depicted
but sometimes you issue deadly fatwas against anyone
who draws a portrait of one of your prophets
You are hard to track down, God
You console and slay with the same warm hand
You turn your visage away from us
when we feel that you have gone too far

And then you suddenly turn up again
a very late night, wrapped in childhood vapors,
smiling a melancholic smile,
grabbing a shaky hand
that has knocked back one too many drinks
Yes, you are indeed hard to track down,
and hard to predict
I am sure you yourself created the trademark
"Inscrutable are the ways of the Lord"
and then you immediately assured yourself of the copyright
to avoid being ripped off by simple counterfeiters
Because you were not born yesterday, God
and you are not stupid
You have made such good plans
and you keep philosophers of all times busy
with the question of how evil can be allowed to
exist in this world
Yes, you have fulfilled many full-time employments
and fed many a sacrificial lamb
And you really have just one tiny little problem;

That you don't exist

But that hasn't stopped others from acting on your behalf

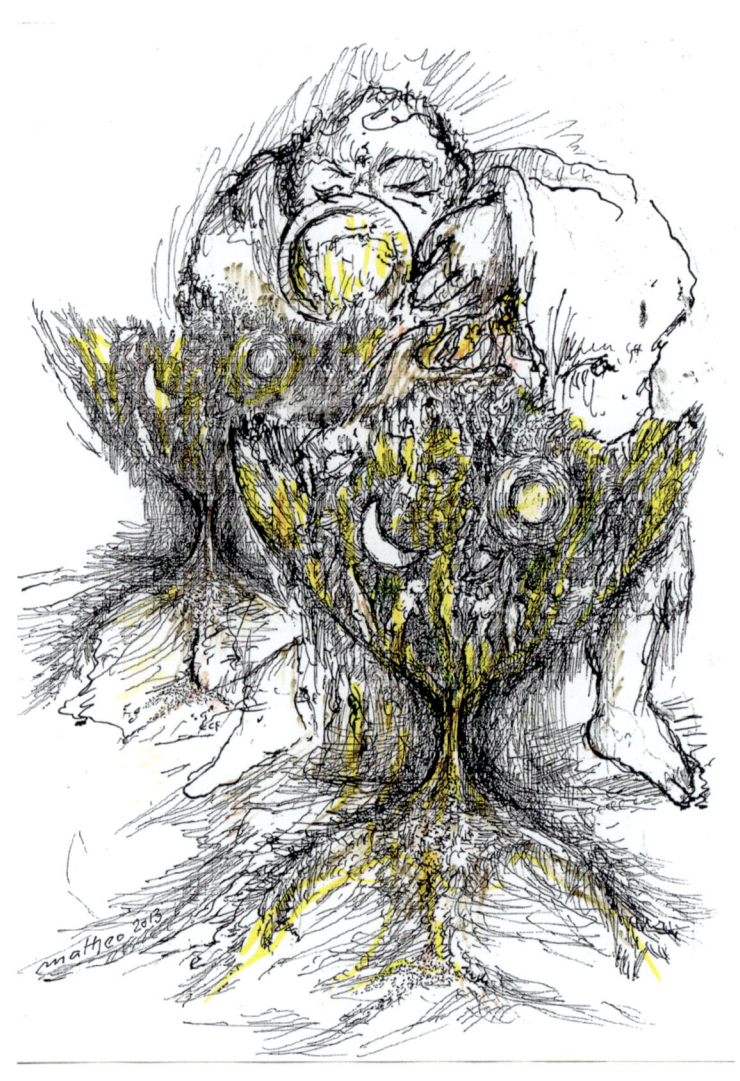

The Chapel

The icons are speaking to this heathen
There is a depth, a weight, a pain
that cannot be rationalized away
Science, logic, thousands of years of misdeeds
in the name of religion, yes…

But then again, this icon in the small chapel
by the beach in Argassi – the eyes, the silence
The chairs that invite to solitary contemplation
when all demands and obligations
are left by the threshold

For a short while the heathen is here
forever the string trembles in his soul

Bougainvillea

They call you bougainvillea
I know
I have seen the biology books
You exist
Have a name
But now you are bleeding yourself
into my morning
Who knows where we will end?
Who writes the new chapters
in the biology books?
Not me
I am totally occupied
by assimilating your unwavering remarks,
your perfectly soundless
red and purple screams
your independance
Who cares about water?
Who cares about Instagram photos?
Who cares about romance?
You sprout, grow and climb
into another lost poet's text

You are seen!
The stone wall stands no chance

The house of senses

You are invited by Kaiti
You take the road northwards from Zante town
It meanders its way up into the mountains
You choose Radio Gamma on the car stereo
sing along with the French chansons
You pass the bay
with the sulphurous water
The horizon follows you along the way
– the sea doesn't interfere with your choice of roads
God has done some Photoshop work
so that the colours match
Then you turn suddenly to the right
into the bumpy road
and you let all your ordinary everyday hassle disappear
as you enter Kaiti's world
The first thing you see are the stones
The second thing you see are the stones
Then you notice that the stones are alive
– they prop wooden beams, hide light bulbs,
open hidden nooks, offer coolness
And then you see the balcony
where Juliet should have been standing
if Romeo had found his way here

- maybe she then would have forgotten her love
in front of the breathtaking sea view,
and Romeo would have left disappointed,
messed around a bit with the pigs and hens
in the neighboring farm,
and then possibly got a lift back to Zante town
But you stay here
You are invited
The dolls welcome you,
the flower painting ask you to step in, take place
in this house of senses
The ingenious arrangements
make your walls against the unexpected crumble
Late at night you sit in the garden
and try to decipher the crickets' excited morse signals
when they discuss your arrival
and share the news over the island;
"The northener has arrived,
his mind's depots need to be replenished,
he has several batteries that need to be charged,
his mental connections are not the very best"
You eat moussaka, drink a cold Mythos beer
You feel the rest of your own being
slowly getting closer to the house:
now your feelings and worries
are by the gate

You await yourself
This is the place where you shall meet!
For a long while you shall sit by Kaiti's house
– even until two and two actually becomes four!

Now the crickets become silent for a short moment

Everybody finally knows that you are here

Liquer store

How can you order
a professional sign
to your shop
and then write Liquer store
instead of Liquor store?
Are there no judicial courts or language squads
that automatically correct these misspellings?
Does this mean that even other things
that seem correct, obvious and unshakable
can be disputed?
I now make an experiment
with the balcony door in solid glass
If I get through
I will write a witty speech
to the Nobel Banquet
in the Stockholm City Hall

The Red Rock

Ina lifts her bow
and plays the initial tones of "Padam padam"
Nikos accompanies her on the piano
The red-dressed waiters hurry between the tables
The Society has gathered again
The poets spin their rosaries
and their words
Sentences are being exchanged, opinions disputed
The sun still scorches the Solomon Square
but Dionysos Solomon himself endures the heat
just as well as ever where he stands
trapped in his statue
A poet knows the heat
but also the coldness when a poem just disappears
into oblivion
The northener I approach the Society
most of the time I sit silent, imbibing the environments
I come from a land far away
where the poets never spin rosaries in their hands
but possibly cocktail glasses
on an annual gathering by the publishing house
Here in Zante The Red Rock is glowing
Culture is close to the surface in the worn paving stones
– all the time new words are born in the short pauses
between the rattling hooves of the tourist horses
and the persistent hummings of the motorbikes

This is the difference – the words,
the language that ramifies between chairs and tables
The northener shuts his eyes, tries to disperse
his inner shyness, tries to forget
his need for loneliness and silence
He hears the violin play, sees the rosaries spin,
feels the ideas bounce like pingpong balls
through the air

The Red Rock is glowing
The Society has gathered again

And Ina always has yet another melody to play